W9-CTW-218

Nate the Great
and The
MISSING
KEY

Nate the Great
and The
MISSING KEY

by Marjorie Weinman Sharmat
illustrations by Marc Simont

A YEARLING BOOK

Published by Yearling, an imprint of Random House Children's Books
a division of Random House, Inc., New York

Visit us on the Web! www.randomhouse.com/kids

Educators and librarians, for a variety of teaching tools, visit us at
www.randomhouse.com/teachers

ISBN: 978-0-440-46191-3

Reprinted by arrangement with the Putnam Publishing Group, Inc.
Printed in the United States of America
One Previous Edition
New Yearling Edition January 2007
61 60 59 58 57

To Mitch,
with love and thanks
for giving me the key
to this mystery

M.W.S.

I, Nate the Great,

am a detective.

I am not afraid of anything.

Except for one thing.

Today I am going

to a birthday party

for the one thing

I am afraid of.

Annie's dog, Fang.

This morning my dog, Sludge,
and I were getting ready
for the party.
The doorbell rang.
I opened the door.
Annie and Fang were standing there.
Fang looked bigger than ever
and so did his teeth.
But he looked like a birthday dog.
He was wearing a stupid sweater
and a new collar.
"I need help," Annie said.
"I can't find the key to my house.
So I can't get inside
to have the birthday party
for Fang."

I, Nate the Great,
was sorry about the key
and glad about the party.
I said,
"Tell me about your key."
"Well," Annie said,

"the last time I saw it

was when I went out

to get Fang a birthday surprise

to eat."

"To eat?" I said.

"Yes," Annie said.

"Some surprise food.
It's the one present
I had forgotten to buy.
I got Fang lots of presents.
A striped sweater.
And a new collar
with a license number,
a name tag,
a little silver dog dish,
and a little silver bone
to hang from the collar.
See how pretty Fang looks
and hear how nicely he jingles."
I, Nate the Great,
did not want
to look at Fang

or listen to him.

"Tell me more," I said.

"Well, Rosamond and her four cats

were at my house," Annie said.

"She was helping me

get ready for the party.

When I went to the store,

I left Rosamond and the cats

in my house.

I left Fang in the yard.

I left the key to my house

on a table.

That is the last time

I saw the key.

When I got back,

Fang was still in the yard.

But the house was locked,

and Rosamond and her cats

were gone.

Rosamond left this note

stuck to my front door."

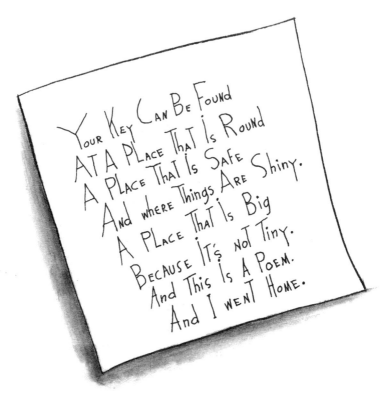

Your Key Can Be Found
At A Place That Is Round
A Place That Is Safe
And where Things Are Shiny.
A Place That Is Big
Because It's Not Tiny.
And This Is A Poem.
And I Went Home.

"That is a strange poem,"

I said.

"Sometimes Rosamond is strange,"

Annie said.

I, Nate the Great,

already knew that.

"You must go

to Rosamond's house

and ask her

where she put your key," I said.

"I went to her house,"

Annie said. "But it was locked, too.

I rang the bell, but no one was home."

"This is a big day

for Rosamond

and locked doors," I said.

"Who else has a key

to your house?"

"My mother and father.

But they went out for the day.

They don't like dog parties,"

Annie said.

I, Nate the Great,

knew that dog parties

are very easy not to like.

But I said,

"I will take your case."

I wrote a note to my mother.

Dear mother,
I am on a case.
I am looking for a round, safe,
shiny, big place.
I do not know where or what
a round, safe, shiny, big place is
But when I find it
I will be back.
Love,
Nate the Great

Annie, Fang, Sludge, and I

went to

Annie's house.

"What does your key look like?"

I asked.

"It is silver and shiny,"
Annie said.

Sludge and I looked around.

There were many places
to leave a key.

Under Annie's doormat.

In her flower garden.

Up her drainpipe.

In her mailbox.

But they were not round,
safe, shiny, and big.

"I will have to look
in other places," I said.

"Fang and I will wait
for you here," Annie said.
I, Nate the Great,
was glad to hear that.

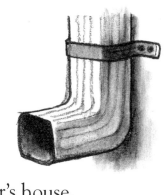

Sludge and I went to Oliver's house.
Oliver is a pest.
But I had a case to solve.
I had a job to do.
I knew that Oliver

collects shiny things.
Like tin cans, safety pins,
badges, poison ivy,
and pictures of the sun.
Each week he collects
one new shiny thing.
Perhaps this week

it was a key.

"Did Rosamond leave a shiny key
with you in a big, round, safe place?"
I asked.

"No," Oliver said.

"This is not my key week.
This is my week
for shiny eels.
Would you like to see
my new eel?"

I, Nate the Great,
did not want to see
a new eel
or an old eel.
I started to leave.

"May I follow you?"

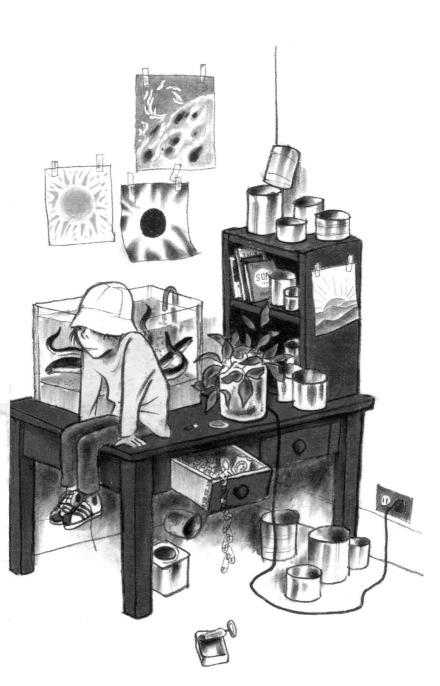

Oliver asked.

"No," I said.

"I will help you look

for the key," Oliver said.

"All right," I said.

"When I go east,

you go west.

When I go south,

you go north."

"But we won't be together,"

Oliver said.

"Exactly," I said.

Sludge and I left Oliver's house.

I did not look back.

I knew what I would see.

Oliver.

I, Nate the Great,
was busy thinking
and looking.
All at once I saw
a big, safe place.
A bank.
I knew there were many
round, shiny things
in a bank.

Like pennies

and nickels

and dimes

and quarters.

Sludge and I walked inside.

Oliver followed us.

Sludge and I looked
on desks and behind counters.
Then we crawled on the floor.
If Rosamond had been here,
there would be cat hairs
all over the floor.

I saw paper clips

and a broken pen

and a penny

and mud.

And a bank guard.

First his feet.

Then the rest of him.

"Do you want

to make a deposit?" he asked.

I, Nate the Great,

wished I could deposit Oliver

in the bank.

I said, "Did anyone strange

with four cats

leave a key here?"

The guard pointed to the door.

Sludge and I left.

Now I, Nate the Great,

knew where I should *not* look

for the key.

A bank was not

a strange enough place

for a strange person like Rosamond

to leave a key.

I had to think of a strange place.

I thought of a kitchen
with bottles of syrup,
hunks of butter,
and stacks of pancakes.
It was not a strange place.
But it was a good place
to think of
because I, Nate the Great,
was hungry.
It was time for lunch.
Sludge and I started for home.

I felt something breathing
on the back of my neck.
I turned around.
It was Oliver.

"I will follow you forever,"
Oliver said.
I, Nate the Great,
knew that forever
was far too long
to be followed
by Oliver.

Sludge and I started to run.

We ran down the street,

up a hill,

around five corners,

and into an alley.

We lost Oliver.

I sat down to rest

beside a garbage can.

Sludge sniffed it.

Sludge likes garbage cans.

I stared at the can.

I had an idea.

A garbage can

would be a perfect place

for Rosamond to hide a key!

It was big and round and shiny

with a shiny cover and shiny handles.
It was safe because no one
would look inside a garbage can.
Except Sludge.
And it was a very strange place
for a key.

Strange enough for Rosamond.
There were not
many places like that.
Now I, Nate the Great,
knew that I had to look
in Annie's garbage can.

Sludge and I walked
to the garbage can
behind Annie's house.
We bent low.
I did not want Annie
to see me
until I found the key
in her garbage can.
Then I would surprise her.
I tried to pull up the cover.
Sludge tried to push up the cover
with his nose.
I pulled harder.
Sludge pushed harder.
The cover came off.
We looked inside the can.

It was empty.

I, Nate the Great,

had not solved the case.

Sludge and I slunk home.

I was very hungry.

I gave Sludge a bone.

I made many pancakes.

I sat down to eat them.

But I did not have a fork.

I opened a drawer.

It was full of spoons and knives

and forks all together

in a shiny silver pile.

I had to pick up

many spoons and knives

before I found a fork.

It is hard to find something

silver and shiny

when it is mixed in

with other things

that are silver and shiny.

I, Nate the Great,

thought about that.

Maybe Annie's key was someplace

where nobody would *see* it

because it was with other

shiny silver things.

A strange place.

A round place.

A big place.

A safe place.

And now I, Nate the Great,

knew the place!

Sludge and I went back

to Annie's house.

Annie was sitting in front

with Fang.

She looked sad.

Fang looked big.

I ran up to Annie.

"I know where your key is,"

I said.

"Where?" Annie asked.

"Look at Fang's collar,"
I said.

Annie looked.

"I see Fang's name tag
hanging from his collar,"
she said. "And his license.
And his silver dog dish.
And his silver bone

and ————————my key!"

"Yes," I said. "I, Nate the Great,
say that Rosamond hung your key
from Fang's collar.
We did not notice it
because there were other

silver things there."

"But why did Rosamond

hang it there?"

Annie asked.

"Well, it is a very strange place,"

I said. "And remember Rosamond's poem.

A *round* place.

A *big* and *safe* place

where things are shiny.

Well, Fang's collar is round.

The things hanging from it

are shiny.

Fang is big.

And safe.

There is no place

more safe

to leave a key

than a few inches

from Fang's teeth.

No one would try

to take off that key.

Including me."

I started to leave.

"Wait!" Annie said.

She took the key

from Fang's collar.

"Now I can have my party

and you can come!"

I, Nate the Great,
was glad for Annie
and sorry for me.
Just then Rosamond
and her four cats
came up the walk.
"You found the key!"
she said. "I knew
I left it in the perfect place."

I, Nate the Great,
had many things
to say to Rosamond.
But the party was starting.
Annie unlocked the door.

We all went inside.

We sat around the birthday table.

Annie gave me

the seat of honor

because I had solved the case.

It was next to Fang.

I, Nate the Great,

hoped it would be

a very short party.

~ Extra ~
Fun Activities!

What's Inside

NATE'S NOTES: Keys

Most adults carry five to ten keys with them whenever they leave home.

Locks and keys have been in use since about 2000 BC. The earliest ones were made of wood. Before keys became common, people hid their valuables behind moats or on islands surrounded by starving crocodiles.

A dead bolt is a common kind of lock. When you turn the key in a dead bolt, the bolt slides into a hole on the doorframe. Inside the cylinder there is a sort of puzzle. Only the right key will solve it. Insert the right key, and its curves and grooves push up a series of pins the exact distance necessary to turn the cylinder—and open the lock!

A remote-controlled lock allows you to open your car door by pushing a button. The "key" transmits a radio signal. Inside the car, a radio receiver gets the message from the "key" to lock or unlock the car.

You can also get a keyless lock for your house. You might press numbers on a keypad to open the lock. Or you might use a plastic card. A really cool keyless lock scans your fingerprint, handprint, or eyeball and then decides whether to let you in.

How many keys exist? To get an idea, think about this: The University of Toronto (in Canada) has more than 100,000 key locks on campus. That's typical for a large university. As Annie discovered, keeping track of keys can be a big job! Still, it's easier than wrestling a starving crocodile or swimming across a moat.

UNIVERSITY OF TORONTO

NATE'S NOTES: Banks

Banks don't like detectives snooping around.
Libraries don't mind. So Nate went to the library
to find out more about banks.

BUREAU OF ENGRAVING AND PRINTING

The U.S. Mint makes pennies, nickels, dimes, quarters, half-dollars, and dollar coins.

Folding money is made at a place called the Bureau of Engraving and Printing.

Every coin or bill made by the government shows the year it was issued. (For more about the dollar bill, see pages 10 to 13.)

The vaults of the Federal Reserve Bank on Maiden Lane in New York City store more than one-quarter of the world's gold. The shiny metal is in the form of bars called bullion.

A Map of a Buck

Here's what you'll find on the front of a dollar bill:

A SEAL:
This seal shows which of the twelve Federal Reserve banks issued the bill. "G" stands for Chicago. (The number 7, shown four times, also stands for Chicago.)

A PORTRAIT:
This is George Washington. He was the first president of the United States.

TWO SIGNATURES: Each bill shows the signatures of the Treasurer of the United States and the Secretary of the Treasury.

A SERIAL NUMBER:
Each bill has a different
number here.

A SPIDER?
Some people claim to
see a spider here.
Other people say
it s actuallly an owl.
What do you see?

Here's what you'll find on the back of a dollar bill:

MDCCLXXVI = 1776:
That was the year of
U.S. independence.

A PYRAMID:
The circle on the left
shows an unfinished
pyramid with thirteen
steps. An eye within a
triangle radiates light.
Weird!

THINK INK:
The back of a dollar bill
is printed with green
ink. That s why some
people call dollars
greenbacks.

12

NOT PAPER:
U.S. folding money is made from cloth, not paper. Red and blue fibers are spread throughout every bill. That helps make it hard to create counterfeit, or fake, money!

A BALD EAGLE:
The eagle is the symbol of America. This one holds thirteen olive branches in one foot and thirteen arrows in the other. The branches stand for peace. The arrows mean war.

How to Make a Fancy Dog (or Cat) Tag

Want to get your dog a present on his birthday?
How about something shiny and round? A new tag!
Cats like them too.

GET TOGETHER:

- card stock or thin cardboard
- scissors
- a hole punch
- markers
- tinfoil
- clear contact paper
- a key ring

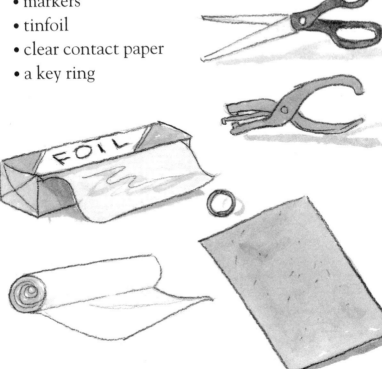

HOW TO MAKE YOUR TAGS:

1. Cut a circle or heart shape out of the card stock or cardboard. Then punch a hole at the top.
2. Decorate one side of the card with a birthday message, like "Happy Birthday" or a drawing of a cake.
3. With a marker, trace the shape onto the tinfoil. Cut it out.

4. Place the shape and the tinfoil together. Enclose them between two pieces of clear contact paper with the sticky sides facing in.
5. Trim the contact paper close to the shape, leaving a little extra on the sides to "glue" the shape and tinfoil together.
6. Clip the tag onto your dog or cat's collar with the key ring.

Funny Pages

Kid: We call our teacher "treasure."
Mom: Why? Do you like her?
Kid: No, we think she should be locked up!

Q: Why did Silly Sam
lock up his pet?
A: *It was a goldfish.*

Q: What happened to a shark that
   swallowed a bunch of keys?
A: *He got lockjaw!*

Q: Why did the football coach go to the bank?

A: *To get his quarterback.*

Q: Why did Silly Sam lock his money in the freezer?

A: *He wanted cold hard cash.*

Q: Where do snowmen keep their money?

A: *In snow banks!*

How to Make a Present Cake

This cake looks like a really awesome present all wrapped up with a bow. It's nice for a pet's birthday party. Or a person's.

Ask an adult to help you with this recipe.

GET TOGETHER:

- one package of cake mix (any flavor)
- the ingredients listed on the cake mix box
- a sheet cake pan
  (usually 9 inches by 13 inches)
- one can of prepared frosting
- a knife
- Fruit by the Foot
- kitchen scissors

MAKE YOUR PRESENT CAKE:

1. Make the sheet cake by following the directions on the box.
2. Allow the cake to cool for at least one hour.
3. Frost the top of the cake.

4. Wrap your cake in "ribbon": Run a piece of Fruit by the Foot down the center of the cake the long way. Trim to fit with the scissors.

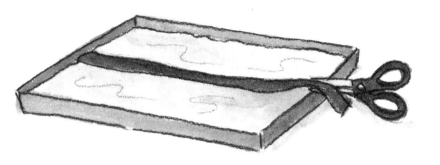

5. Now run another piece of Fruit by the Foot across the width of the cake. Trim to fit. When you're finished, your cake should look something like this:

6. Make the "bow." Use the Fruit by the Foot to make three long loops. You'll need one big one (about as long as your forearm) and two medium ones (about as long as your hand). Put the longer piece in the middle of the other two and squish the centers together like this:

7. Now make two circles, about the size of golf balls. Place the circles on either side of the loops. Run another short piece of Fruit by the Foot around the loops and through the center of each circle so that all the pieces are pulled together, like this:

8. Place the "bow" on top of the cake.

9. Make the ribbon tails. Cut two more pieces of Fruit by the Foot. Cut one end of each into a V shape. Place the plain ends of the ribbon tails under the "bow."

10. Serve while singing "Happy Birthday."

♪ Happy Birthday to You! ♫

11. Enjoy!

More Funny Pages

Doctor, Doctor, Fang's birthday cake gave me heartburn!
Next time don't eat the candles!

Q: What did Fang's birthday party end with?
A: *A Y!*

Q: What does Fang always get on his birthday?
A: *Another year older!*

Q: What do you give Fang on his birthday?
A: *I don't know, but you'd better hope he likes it.*

Q: Why do we put candles on the top of a birthday cake?
A: *Because it's too hard to put them on the bottom!*

More Ways to Make Your Pet's Birthday Special*

Start the day with a special treat. Is your dog wild about bones? Does your kitty covet liver? Today is the day to go out of your way and provide a yummy breakfast for your furry, feathered, or scaly friend.

Play dress-up. Get into a party mood by putting a bow on your bird's cage or on your fish's aquarium. Your dog or cat may be willing to wear a birthday hat or a special bow on her collar—at least for a few minutes.

Spend a little time. Toss the ball to your retriever, or give your kitty a good belly rub. Make a little extra time for your pet's favorite activity.

Invite a friend. If your pet is the social type, invite a friend to meet you at the park or at your house.

Record the big day. Take photos of your birthday boy or girl. Or make a special piece of art to celebrate the occasion.

*If you don't know your pet's birthday, you can celebrate the day he joined your family!

Have you helped solve all Nate the Great's mysteries?

❑ **Nate the Great**: Meet Nate, the great detective, and join him as he uses incredible sleuthing skills to solve his first big case.

❑ **Nate the Great Goes Undercover**: Who— or what—is raiding Oliver's trash every night? Nate bravely hides out in his friend's garbage can to catch the smelly crook.

❑ **Nate the Great and the Lost List**: Nate loves pancakes, but who ever heard of cats eating them? Is a strange recipe at the heart of this mystery?

❑ **Nate the Great and the Phony Clue**: Against ferocious cats, hostile adversaries, and a sly phony clue, Nate struggles to prove that he's still the world's greatest detective.

❑ **Nate the Great and the Sticky Case**: Nate is stuck with his stickiest case yet as he hunts for his friend Claude's valuable stegosaurus stamp.

❑ **Nate the Great and the Missing Key**: Nate isn't afraid to look anywhere—even under the nose of his friend's ferocious dog, Fang—to solve the case of the missing key.

- **Nate the Great and the Snowy Trail**: Nate has his work cut out for him when his friend Rosamond loses the birthday present she was going to give him. How can he find the present when Rosamond won't even tell him what it is?

- **Nate the Great and the Fishy Prize**: The trophy for the Smartest Pet Contest has disappeared! Will Sludge, Nate's clue-sniffing dog, help solve the case and prove he's worthy of the prize?

- **Nate the Great Stalks Stupidweed**: When his friend Oliver loses his special plant, Nate searches high and low. Who knew a little weed could be so tricky?

- **Nate the Great and the Boring Beach Bag**: It's no relaxing day at the beach for Nate and his trusty dog, Sludge, as they search through sand and surf for signs of a missing beach bag.

- **Nate the Great Goes Down in the Dumps**: Nate discovers that the only way to clean up this case is to visit the town dump. Detective work can sure get dirty!

- **Nate the Great and the Halloween Hunt**: It's Halloween, but Nate isn't trick-or-treating for candy. Can any of the witches, pirates, and robots he meets help him find a missing cat?

- **Nate the Great and the Musical Note**: Nate is used to looking for clues, not listening for them! When he gets caught in the middle of a musical riddle, can he hear his way out?

❑ **Nate the Great and the Stolen Base**: It's not easy to track down a stolen base, and Nate's hunt leads him to some strange places before he finds himself at bat once more.

❑ **Nate the Great and the Pillowcase**: When a pillowcase goes missing, Nate must venture into the dead of night to search for clues. Everyone sleeps easier knowing Nate the Great is on the case!

❑ **Nate the Great and the Mushy Valentine**: Nate hates mushy stuff. But when someone leaves a big heart taped to Sludge's doghouse, Nate must help his favorite pooch discover his secret admirer.

❑ **Nate the Great and the Tardy Tortoise**: Where did the mysterious green tortoise in Nate's yard come from? Nate needs all his patience to follow this slow . . . slow . . . clue.

❑ **Nate the Great and the Crunchy Christmas**: It's Christmas, and Fang, Annie's scary dog, is not feeling jolly. Can Nate find Fang's crunchy Christmas mail before Fang crunches on *him*?

❑ **Nate the Great Saves the King of Sweden**: Can Nate solve his *first-ever* international case without leaving his own neighborhood?

❑ **Nate the Great and Me: The Case of the Fleeing Fang**: A surprise Happy Detective Day party is great fun for Nate until his friend's dog disappears! Help Nate track down the missing pooch, and learn all the tricks of the trade in a special fun section for aspiring detectives.

❏ **Nate the Great and the Monster Mess**: Nate loves his mother's deliciously spooky Monster Cookies, but the recipe has vanished! This is one case Nate and his growling stomach can't afford to lose.

❏ **Nate the Great, San Francisco Detective**: Nate visits his cousin Olivia Sharp in the big city, but it's no vacation. Can he find a lost joke book in time to save the world?

❏ **Nate the Great and the Big Sniff**: Nate depends on his dog, Sludge, to help him solve all his cases. But Nate is on his own this time, because Sludge has disappeared! Can Nate solve the case and recover his canine buddy?

❏ **Nate the Great on the Owl Express**: Nate boards a train to guard Hoot, his cousin Olivia Sharp's pet owl. Then Hoot vanishes! Can Nate find out *whooo* took the feathered creature?